Photographic Memory

Story *by* **Ron Bunney**

Illustrations *by* **Richard Hoit**

PM Chapter Books

Emerald Level 27 Set A

U.S. Edition © 2013 Houghton Mifflin Harcourt Publishing Company
125 High Street
Boston, MA 02110
www.hmhco.com

Text © 2001 Cengage Learning Australia Pty Limited
Illustrations © 2001 Cengage Learning Australia Pty Limited
Originally published in Australia by Cengage Learning Australia

21   1957   19
28352

Text: Ron Bunney
Illustrations: Richard Hoit
Printed in China by 1010 Printing International Ltd

Photographic Memory
ISBN 978 0 76 357785 8

Contents

Chapter 1
The Giant Camel

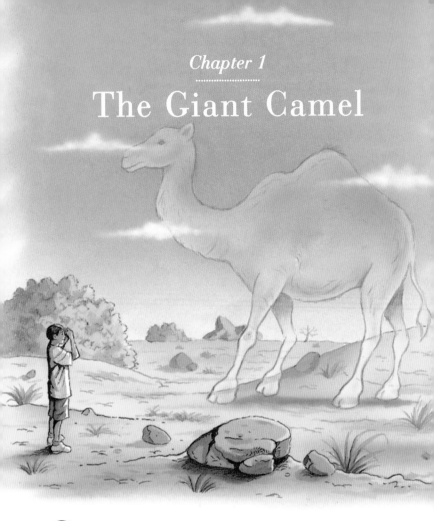

Sam couldn't believe it. Was that a thirty-foot tall camel walking toward him? He ran toward it. Then he skidded to a stop and pulled his brand new digital camera out of his pocket. It was a gift for his eleventh birthday.

Sam lined up the camel in the viewfinder of the camera, and he snapped the shot. Then Sam charged off again. Everything he saw was new and strange. This was his third day of traveling in the outback of Australia with his family and living in a rented camper. He was exploring the area as his parents prepared lunch.

Sam ran past a small pile of earth and rocks further away from the camper. He wanted to get a picture of that gigantic camel from another angle. Surely these pictures would make him famous. He jogged down a slope and out into a vast area of low scrub. It was very hot, but he kept on going.

Puffing and panting, Sam paused to wipe the sweat from his eyes. They were stinging and felt rather strange. Sam felt very confused. The camel had shrunk. He rubbed his eyes again.

Oh no! As Sam looked more closely, he realized the giant camel was only a mirage! It wasn't real at all. Then he remembered his photo. He used the tiny screen on the back of the camera to study the image that had been recorded in the camera's memory.

There was a shape. But was it a camel? Sam had certainly been hoping to see some camels. Perhaps he had imagined it.

Sighing loudly, Sam put the camera back in his pocket. It wouldn't make him famous, but at least it showed the sort of country they were traveling through. He would show it to his grandparents when he got back to Iowa. Otherwise they would never believe that the earth could be so red.

Chapter 2

Time for Lunch

Sam looked around him. The day seemed to be getting even hotter, and he had been away quite a long time. It was time to get back to his parents and have lunch. Sam remembered that he had come past a small rock formation. Yes, that was it over there.

He started back. The sun beat down, and he wished he'd worn the hat his mother was always telling him to wear. But he hadn't meant to come so far. He should have brought the water bottle his father had given him. In this heat he really wanted some ice-cold water. Sam tried to swallow, but his throat felt too dry.

The heat was building up in him. His body felt like a sponge, absorbing heat. The open country made it hard to figure out distances, and the rocky mound was farther away than he thought. He finally reached it, but then he came to a stop!

Sam stared. Where was the trail? Where was the camper? It must be around the other side. He would soon check.

He climbed onto the rocks and gazed around in amazement. All he could see was miles of scrub, an occasional tree, and many more oddly shaped, rocky mounds.

Suddenly he was full of doubt. He didn't know what to do.

Then Sam took a deep breath and looked again. He had to find his parents! Perhaps the trail was on the other side of the next rock? Scrambling down, he set off toward it, trying to feel confident. The rocks all looked alike. It was easy to make a mistake.

As he walked, he remembered something his father had once told him. "When you are hiking in unfamiliar country, turn around as you leave and look at your basecamp. Study it and see what it looks like from that direction. It will help you find your way back to camp."

Sam felt hollow inside. Rushing off as he had, he had forgotten his father's words of advice.

Chapter 3

Lost!

As he plodded on under the hot sun, Sam thought about some of the other stories his father had told him, stories about earlier trips to other countries. This was the first time Sam and his mother had gone on a trip with his father.

Sam's father knew a lot about survival skills and had passed this knowledge on to his son. "You never know when you might need it," he would say. Unfortunately, Sam had not really listened. Now he wished he had been more attentive.

Sighing, Sam looked down and realized that he was at the edge of a dry water hole. As he stepped into it, he suddenly felt very afraid.

Sam knew he hadn't crossed any water holes when he left the camper. He was lost! He felt very scared and very lonely.

He flopped down to the ground in the shade of a tree. All he wanted was a drink, his mouth was so dry. The sun was directly overhead and this made Sam even more worried. He was sure that he had headed west when he left the trail.

If it was late afternoon, then the sun would be low in the west and he could have figured out where east was and gone in that direction.

He squinted at the sun. All it told him was that it was lunchtime, but the hollow feeling inside him wasn't caused by hunger.

With shoulders slumped, Sam sat and stared at the dry earth. He didn't know what to do. The sun's heat was so fierce it frightened him. Suddenly all Sam wanted was to be home again.

Chapter 4
All Alone

The desert was not friendly. It had lots of surprises and wonderful things to see, but it could be very dangerous as well. Sam's lip trembled and tears formed in his eyes. Then he jerked upright. He wasn't going to cry! Anger pumped through him. There was no way he was going to lie down and give in.

He jumped to his feet and scanned three hundred and sixty degrees. At least he remembered to do that from his father's stories. He knew all about compasses and angles.

There were rocky mounds all around him, but some looked too big, and others too small. He couldn't recognize any of them.

He wished, again, that he had carefully studied the one he had started from. He looked at the small trees nearby. If he climbed one, it should give him a better view. Moving slowly because of the heat, Sam started to climb the tallest tree. But it was no good. The lowest branches would not hold his weight, and he fell, cutting his shin.

Back on the ground, Sam tied his handkerchief over his bleeding leg to keep the flies away. Then he made a decision. He would head toward the highest mound. Once on top, he would be able to see farther and get a better picture of the whole area. After that he would know which way to go!

On the hike to the highest mound, the heat sucked more energy and moisture from his body. Sam crawled the last few yards to the top of the mound. Once on top of it, he couldn't believe his eyes. There was still no sign of the trail. The sun poured down on him from above. He had to find his parents.

Stumbling down, Sam saw a large piece of flat rock sticking out near the base of the mound. He went to investigate it. It formed a small cave and it offered shade. He crawled inside. It was much cooler here than it was up on top of the rocks.

Sam's pulse pounded, and he wondered where the sweat came from. He didn't think there was any moisture left in his body.

He lay on his side in the cool shade. He'd rest for a few minutes, then figure out where to go. Rolling onto his back, he lay with his arms by his side. He had seen his father do that when he wanted to think. Less than half a yard on his right was the back wall of the small cave. There was a ledge a little above his face. He glanced at it and then froze!

A coiled snake lay on the ledge with its head raised. Its body was arched, ready to strike. The snake's hard eyes stared at him as its forked tongue darted in and out.

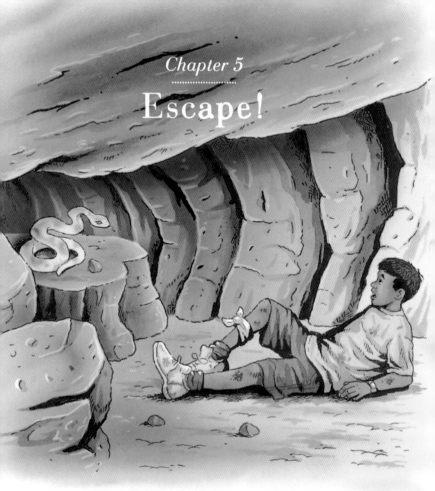

Chapter 5

Escape!

Sam wanted to yell for his father, or run away, or do anything but lie there! But common sense told him to keep absolutely still. Any quick movement might make the snake strike. Sam was on his own—there was no one who could help him. He didn't know what he should do.

The fingers of his left hand curled in the cool sand. If only he could sink all the way into it!

Sam took a slow, deep breath and tried to remember what he had been told to do if he saw a snake. He looked at the snake from the corner of his eye and hoped it was as scared as he was.

Then as quickly and quietly as he could, he backed out of the cave, keeping his movement as smooth as possible.

Once outside the cave, Sam leaped to his feet and ran away from the mound before stopping and checking to see if he was all right. He looked around the edges of a nearby rock, then climbed up and sat on it.

Sam sat with his knees under his chin, keeping his feet clear of the ground. He tried to relax his muscles. Why was he shivering in such heat?

If only he could see the rocky mound he had found near the trail. There must be something different about the one he'd started from.

Then Sam remembered. He'd jogged down the slope after taking the photograph. He could use the photograph to help him remember!

He pulled the camera out of his pocket and stared at the image on the screen. Hope surged in his mind. There was something he wanted to remember, but he didn't know what it was. Then this tiny bit of hope faded as he lifted his head and gazed at the country around him. He could have taken fifty photos and they would all look exactly the same.

Suddenly Sam had a new idea. Carefully watching for snakes, he climbed back to the top of the mound. From its highest point, he scanned a full three hundred and sixty degrees.

After he had looked in every direction, he chose the most likely one. He held the camera slightly below his eyes and looked at the image. Then he looked at the distant section of scrub land. He stared down again at the image and then quickly back at the actual view.

Sam thought as hard as he could. He had a picture in his mind of the first rock formation he had passed. The rock on the very top had been unusually smooth. He could see the same rock in the very corner of the photograph.

Now all he needed to do was to find the same shaped rock.

Chapter 6

Back to Camp

Sam turned slowly again. This time he studied each rock formation, trying to find the familiar rock. He stopped. He could see it! He looked down at the digital image and across to the rock. They matched! He set off toward the rock, holding the camera in front of him like a map.

Sam walked confidently in the direction of the rock.

Every few minutes he stopped and checked his direction, keeping the distant rock firmly in his sight.

Now Sam's energy was almost gone. He was exhausted. Somehow, he kept his feet moving and his eyes gazing at the rock. It was not far now.

From behind the rocks, Sam could see something that looked like smoke rising into the air.

His heart sped up. Was it real? Or another mirage? He didn't know.

He rubbed his eyes and squinted through the heat haze. There was a shadow in the distance. It was his father running toward him!

Relief flowed through Sam like a cool breeze. He was back at camp and he'd figured out how to get back himself, using only a photograph. It was lucky for him that his new digital camera had a photographic memory!